ISBN: 0-7172-8765-3

Manufactured in the United States of America.
A B C D   1 2 3 4

WALT DISNEY's

The Fox and the Hound

GROLIER
BOOK CLUB EDITION

One spring morning, a mother fox dashed through a meadow carrying her baby. A hunter and his dogs were chasing them, and the mother fox needed to find a safe place to hide her cub.

The mother fox soon came to a patch of tall grass. She covered up her baby and ran away hoping that the dogs would follow her. The dogs came sniffing through the grass, but they did not see the frightened baby fox.

When the hunter and his dogs disappeared, the baby fox poked his tiny nose out of the grass and sniffed around. The little fox waited and waited, but there was no sign of his mother.

Luckily, a kindly owl named Big Mama had seen everything. She flew down to comfort the little fox.

"Now, don't you worry," said the gentle owl. "Big Mama will find someone to take care of you."

Big Mama quickly found
her two friends, Dinky the
sparrow and Boomer the
woodpecker.

"Please help me," said
Big Mama. "We must find a
new home for this little fox."

Dinky and Boomer had been
trying to catch a caterpillar
for their dinner, but they
stopped to help Big Mama.

"What can we do to help
the little fellow?" they asked,
while the caterpillar quietly
crawled away.

"We'll lead that nice Widow Tweed right to him," Big Mama explained. "She'll know what to do after that."

And so Big Mama and Boomer grabbed a piece of Widow Tweed's washing from her clothesline. When the widow ran after the birds, they dropped the clothing right on top of the baby fox.

"Goodness!" cried Widow Tweed when she
spotted the baby fox. "What are you doing here?"

The warmhearted widow loved the little fox at once. "You're just like a toddler," said Widow Tweed. "I think I will call you Tod for short." Tod liked the widow and his new name very much.

Not far from the widow's house lived a hunter named Amos. He had just come home with a puppy.

"His name is Copper," Amos told his old dog Chief. "He'll be a big help to us when he grows up."

But Chief did not want any help and he pretended not to care about Copper.

When Copper curled up beside Chief and fell asleep, Chief decided the puppy wasn't so bad, after all.

As Copper grew up, he became very curious about the world around him. One day, as he went sniffing through the forest…

...he found himself nose-to-nose with a fox!

"My name is Copper," said the puppy.
"My name is Tod," said the little fox.

And before the day was over, the fox and the hound were the best of friends.

That evening, Amos the hunter was very angry when Copper came home. He decided to tie up Copper, so that the puppy could not get away from his doghouse again.

Tod hid in the bushes and watched. He was very sad to see his new friend in trouble.

Tod decided to visit
his friend to cheer him
up. But as soon as Chief
smelled the fox he began
to chase him.

When Amos saw Chief chasing
Tod, the hunter was sure Tod
was after his chickens. So Amos
chased Tod all the way to
Widow Tweed's house.

"You keep that fox away from my chickens!" Amos shouted angrily at Widow Tweed.

"You leave Tod alone!" Widow Tweed declared. "He would never hurt your chickens! Now go away!"

Tod was very frightened,
and so was the widow. She
knew that Tod would get hurt
if he went near Amos's
property again.

"Tod, you'd better stay in the house," she said sadly.

A few days later, Tod watched from Widow Tweed's
window as Amos packed for a hunting trip. Tod was
even sadder when he saw his friend Copper disappear
from view as Amos drove away.

As the weeks passed, Copper learned how
to be a hunting dog just like Chief.

Soon Copper was no longer a puppy,
but a full-grown dog with a nose that
could track anything!

Back home, Tod grew tired of waiting for Copper to come back. He decided to pay a visit to Amos's house to see if they had returned.

On the way he ran into his old friend Big Mama. "Be careful," she warned. "Copper is grown up, just like you. His job is to chase foxes now. He can't be your friend anymore."

Tod didn't believe Copper could have changed so much.

At last Copper came home. He sat in the
front seat with Amos, howling as only a
dog can howl. Chief just covered his ears.

That night, Tod heard Copper's howling and ran over
to greet his pal.

Copper was surprised to see Tod, but sadly told him
to go away.

"We can't be the best of friends anymore," Copper
tried to explain. "I have a job to do, and that job is to
hunt foxes!"

Tod tried to argue, but Chief suddenly began to bark.

Tod tried to get away from Chief. He zigzagged as fast as he could, but another dog was right behind him. It was Copper! The dogs had gotten loose!

"I won't let him find you," Copper barked. "Run to the bridge. I'll lead him the other way."

But Chief was a smart old hunting dog. He was
waiting for Tod on the bridge. Moments later, a
rumble surprised them both. Chief and Tod looked
up to see a train coming at them full speed!

Tod squeezed into a tiny
space as the train roared past.
But Chief was not so lucky. He
was forced right off the bridge
by the speeding train.

When Copper found Chief, he blamed Tod. "This is what happens when you're friends with a fox," he thought angrily. "I won't let him get away again."

Tod was very frightened. As soon as he
returned home, he curled up in Widow Tweed's
arms. Suddenly Amos pounded on the door.

"Your fox almost got my dog killed tonight!"
Amos shouted at the window. "He's a nasty,
wild animal!"

Widow Tweed shouted back at Amos. *"You're*
the nasty one! Leave us alone!"

Widow Tweed knew Amos was right about Tod being
a wild animal. He didn't belong on a farm any longer.
He needed to be free.

She brought Tod to
a safe place in the
woods and hugged him.

"This will be your
home now, Tod," she
said sadly. "It will be
better for you here."
Tod watched her go,
feeling very lonely
and sad.

But he wasn't alone for long. His old friend Big
Mama was watching out for him, and she led him
to a lovely lady fox named Vixey.

Soon Tod had a new best friend!

One day the two young foxes heard gunshots.
It was Amos and Copper out hunting.
"Run, Vixey!" Tod shouted as they dashed away.

The loud growl of a bear interrupted the chase.
Suddenly the angry bear rushed toward all of
them. Shocked, Amos stepped back—right into
a steel trap!

Copper bravely tried to protect his master,
but the tough old bear threw the faithful dog
to the ground.

Tod stopped running when he heard Copper's barking. "Copper tried to help me once," he remembered. He raced back to try to save his old friend from the angry bear.

The bear forgot about Copper as he chased Tod
to the river. Tod tried to escape across an old log,
but when the bear followed him, the log broke.
Tod and the bear plunged into the cold
water below!

Tod pulled himself to the shore, only to find Amos aiming his gun right at him!

Copper couldn't let Amos hurt Tod. Quickly, he stood in Amos's way, protecting his friend.

Amos lowered his gun. "You're right," he said. "The fox saved us from the bear." Copper then went and stood by Amos as they watched Tod escape.

When Widow Tweed saw Amos limping home, she hurried out to see what had happened. As she bandaged his hurt foot, Amos told her about Tod, Copper, and the bear.

"I was wrong," said Amos. "Your fox is nice, after all."

Widow Tweed just smiled. She knew Tod would be safe from Amos from now on.

A few days later, Tod and
Vixey sat on a cliff over-
looking the valley. They
looked down at their friends
and wished them happiness.

"Now I know what the
two most beautiful things in
the world are," Tod told Vixey.
"Love and friendship."

Tod and Vixey agreed that
they were lucky to have both.